W9-BNA-939

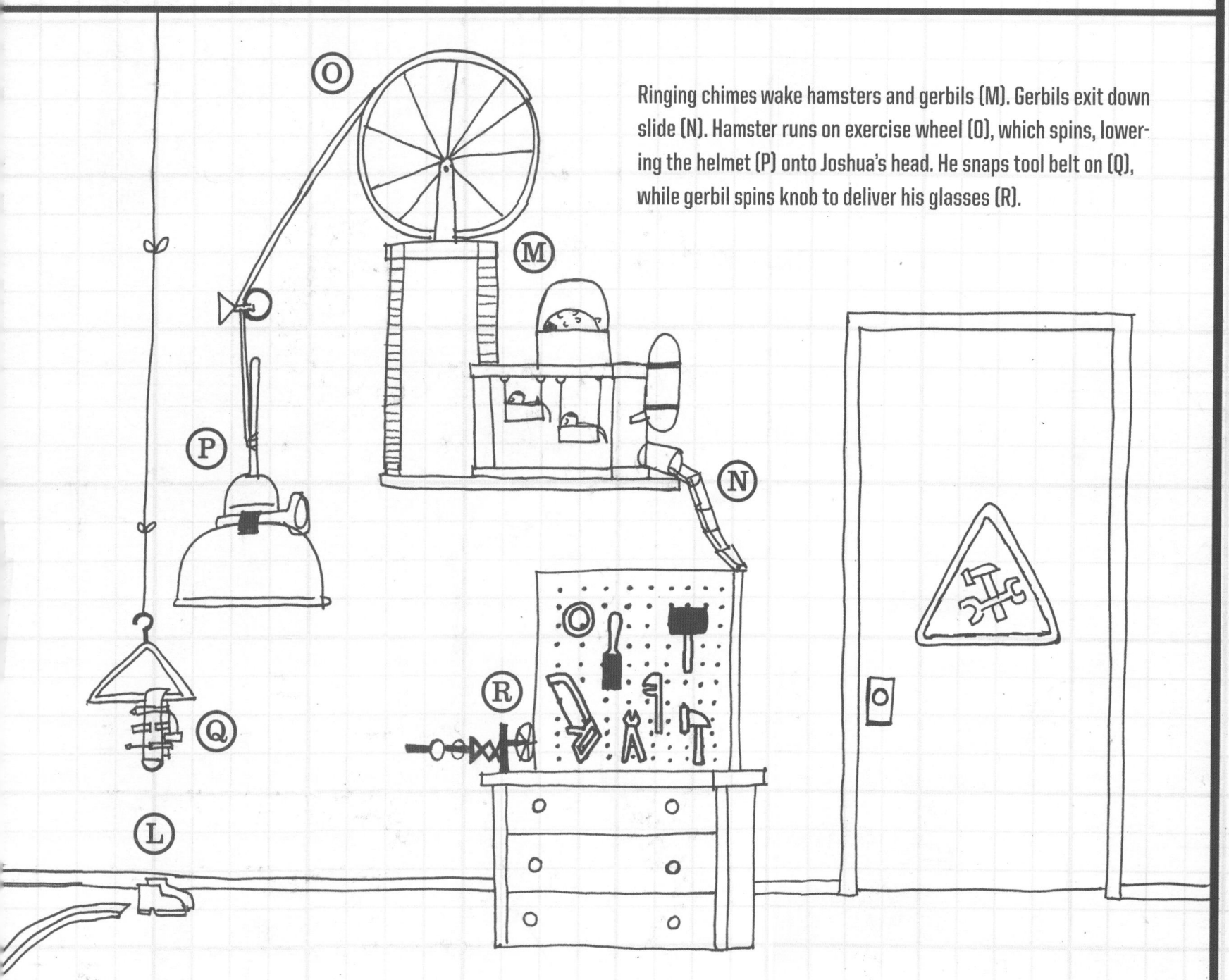

Ringing chimes wake hamsters and gerbils (M). Gerbils exit down slide (N). Hamster runs on exercise wheel (O), which spins, lowering the helmet (P) onto Joshua's head. He snaps tool belt on (Q), while gerbil spins knob to deliver his glasses (R).

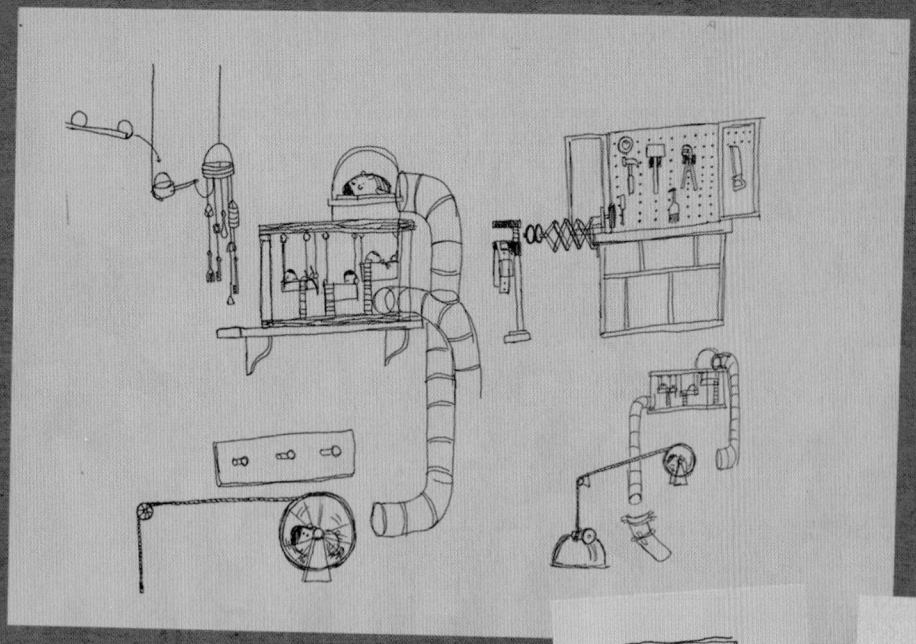

The Fix-It Man
Text copyright © 2016 by Susan Hood
Illustrations copyright © 2016 by Arree Chung
All rights reserved. Manufactured in China.
No part of this book may be used or reproduced in any manner whatsoever without
written permission except in the case of brief quotations embodied in critical articles and reviews.
For information address HarperCollins Children's Books, a division of
HarperCollins Publishers, 195 Broadway, New York, NY 10007.

www.harpercollinschildrens.com

ISBN 978-0-06-237085-3 (trade bdg.)

The artist used paper collage, duct tape, string, watercolors, ink, and
Photoshop to create the illustrations for this book.
16 17 18 19 20 SCP 10 9 8 7 6 5 4 3 2 1
❖
First Edition

Words by Susan Hood
Pictures by Arree Chung

HARPER
An Imprint of HarperCollins*Publishers*

He snaps his tool belt,
dons his hat.

He swings his hammer—
RAT-
A-
TAT-
TAT!

He pounds a peg

and turns a screw,
but that's not all
that he can do.

When things conk out or crash or crack,
he tinkers till they're back on track.
Fix a flat?
E = MC²
ZZZ...

Repair a wreck?
ZZ
CRASH!

ZZ
ZOOM!

Build a bridge?
CHECK
CHECK
AND
CHECK!

With Joshua James, it won't take long to look around and fix what's wrong.
!!!
#
@/#
@#/☆!
✓ check
✓ check
✓ check!

P.U. Those diapers sure do stink.
Clipboard out! It's time to think!

No job's too big,
beyond repair,

but some require extra care.

The wheels are turning—plan's in place!
The Fix-It Man is on the case!
SNAP!

SOPHIE

SNAP!
SOPHIE
If one solution just won't do,
SOPHIE

the Fix-It Man
can try Fix Two.
SOPHIE
A
B
C

Some fixes

may not go as planned . . .

H
I
J
K
L
ZZ zz

but J.J.'s there to lend a hand!
!!!
@!#

At times like these, you may have heard,
the best fix is a single word!

Sorry!
H
I

Success! The system is a go.
Here they come! Look out below!

Bye-bye, diapers, so long, smell,
Toodle-oo, ta-ta, farewell!
L
K
J

Let's hear it for the Fix-It Man.
That stinky problem's in the can!

NAILED IT!
M
N

Well, almost. . . .
!
WHACK!
SQUAWK!
WHOA!
WHOOPS!

Everyone goofs, and things can break.
Even dads can make mistakes!

A helping hand, a hug or two
will fix him up as good as new.
Uh-oh!
Look out!

One never knows just how or why
new problems tumble from the sky.

No fix-it tricks can mend this crack.
The deed is done—no going back!
So if a fix leaves you perplexed,
wait and see . . .

what happens next!

Things may need to break in two
to bring the world something new!

OPERATION: DUMP THE DIAPERS

Toy crane lifts diaper from diaper pail (A) and drops on ramp (B), where it slides down to train car (C). Train carries diaper to gerbil's forklift (D). He lifts it to Ferris wheel car (E). Diaper rides up belt (F) and is hooked by paper clip (G). It travels until scissors clip it (H) and it falls to ramp (I) below.